# Our Mitzvah Muscles and other stories

by Menucha Fuchs

THE JUDAICA PRESS, INC.

*Our Mitzvah Muscles and other stories*
© 2010 The Judaica Press, Inc.

ISBN: 978-1-60763-031-9


THE JUDAICA PRESS, INC.
123 Ditmas Avenue / Brooklyn, NY 11218
718-972-6200 / 800-972-6201
info@judaicapress.com
www.judaicapress.com


*Manufactured in the United States of America*

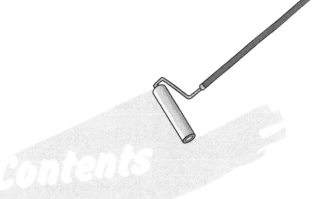

## Contents

# 107 | Children's Stories About Friendship

# Meet the Cohen Family

**Ruti:** It's not easy being the oldest of ten children, but if anyone can do it, eighteen-year-old Ruti can!

**Zisi:** Fifteen-year-old Zisi always goes out of her way to help anyone—whether it's a member of her family, a friend or even a stranger.

**Mordechai:** Twelve-year-old Mordechai is the oldest of the Cohen boys. Though not yet bar mitzvah, Mordechai takes his responsibilities very seriously and thinks of himself as Abba's main helper.

**Rina:** Eleven-year-old Rina would like to keep up with her older sisters and often plans to do "grown up" things with Zisi. She also loves talking to and playing with her friends.

**Efrayim:** Nine-year-old Efrayim is friendly, helpful and very studious. He wears thick glasses and can barely see without them.

**Eliezer:** Curious and mischievous, seven-year-old Eliezer enjoys experimenting and exploring his world.

**Miri:** Adorable Miri is three-years-old. She always makes sure her brothers and sisters know she is there—even when they try to ignore her!

**Naftali:** Though only two-years-old, Naftali already thinks of himself as a "big boy."

**Penina:** One-year-old Penina is the youngest girl in the Cohen family.

… And the newest member of the family: another little brother, **Yoni!**

THE CHILDREN'S LEARNING SERIES

CHILDREN'S STORIES ABOUT

CHESSED

BY MENUCHA FUCHS · ILLUSTRATED BY YONI

# A Medicine Gemach

It was Friday night. The candles were still burning as we sat in the dining room and Abba told us stories about great rabbis from long ago. Penina, my one-year-old baby sister, sat on Ima's lap and laughed.

I love being with my family on Friday nights. It's so quiet and everyone is always so happy. Abba tells us divrei Torah and stories, and little Penina just sits there giggling.

Just like clockwork, every Friday night, two-year-old Naftali falls asleep at the table. Ima carries him to his room and helps him put on his pajamas. Miri follows them and goes to bed, too. Abba continues to tell us stories. When he sees my eyes closing, he says, "Mordechai, it's time for bed." I run into my bed, say Shema Yisrael, cover myself with my blanket and fall asleep.

This Friday night was different. As I pulled the blanket over my head, I heard loud cries. At first, I thought there was a cat in our yard. But when Ima began to rock Penina's bed, I knew it was Penina who was crying. Ima took Penina's temperature. It was very high, and Ima was worried. When she gave Penina her medicine, Penina licked the spoon and stopped crying. Soon the room was quiet and I fell asleep.

Later that night, Penina began to cry again. I got up and looked outside. It was still dark. The Shabbos candles had burned out and I couldn't see anything. I heard Abba and Ima talking. I knew they were worried, so I got out of bed and went to the living room.

The street lamp lit up the room. Ima was sitting on the sofa and holding Penina. Abba was standing near the window. When Penina saw me, she tried to smile. But soon she began to cry again. She picked up her hand and put it on her ear.

"I think her ear hurts," Ima said.

Ima asked me to hold Penina and went to look for more medicine. She came back with the medicine bottle, but it was empty.

"What should we do?" she asked.

"I have an idea," I said. "We can go to Rabbi Pollack's house. He has a medicine *gemach*. He doesn't live far away. But do you think we can knock on his door now? It's very late."

"We have no choice," Ima said sadly.

"What's wrong with Penina?" I asked.

"She's sick and she can't sleep," Abba said.

I got dressed quickly, and Abba and I hurried to Rabbi Pollack's house. The streets were completely empty. The houses were all dark. Only the street lamps shone.

We reached Rabbi Pollack's house. The street lamp was near his door and we saw his name on the mailbox. Near the mailbox was

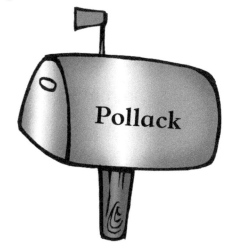

a small sign that said: *"Medicine Gemach. Open 24 hours a day. Refuah Sheleimah!"*

Medicine Gemach
Open 24 hours a day
Refuah Sheleimah!

"Did you see that sign?" Abba asked in surprise.

"Yes!" I answered happily.

We hurried up the steps and knocked on Rabbi Pollack's door.

We knocked quietly, because we thought the Pollacks would be sleeping. No one answered. We knocked a second time, then a third. At last someone asked: "Who's there?"

"I'm sorry for coming so late, but my baby is running a high fever," Abba said.

The door opened. Rabbi Pollack was wearing a robe.

"Can I help you?" he asked.

"I need some medicine for my daughter. I'm sorry we woke you," Abba said.

"Don't worry," Rabbi Pollack replied. "It's a mitzvah to help people! Please come in."

We came inside and Rabbi Pollack went to another room. Soon he came back out with a small bottle of medicine. It came with a dropper, to make it easy to give the medicine to a little child.

"Here, this should help you. I hope your daughter feels better soon!" He wished us a good Shabbos and waved good-bye.

Abba and I walked home silently. Ima met us at the door, took the bottle and gave Penina some medicine. Then we all went to bed.

The next morning, my head hurt a little. But I got out of bed because I didn't want to be late for Shacharis. When I passed by Rabbi

Pollack's house, I ran over to the mailbox and read the small sign over and over again. A wonderful feeling filled my heart.

*Jews are so kind!* I thought. *They have such good hearts, and they want to help others even in the middle of the night on Shabbos. Who knows what would have happened to Penina without this medicine! I'm so proud to be a Jew!*

# The Lost Children Gemach

"Can I take Naftali with me?" I asked Ima.

"Where are you going?" she asked.

"To Avigdor's house," I answered. "Naftali can come along. Avigdor's little brothers will play with him. There is a small slide in the park near his house, and a sandbox, too."

"Fine," Ima said. "I have to go shopping

and will come back in about an hour. Ruti can stay home with the little ones."

Ima left. I took Naftali's hand and went to Avigdor's house.

Many children were playing in the park.

"Do you want to play with them?" I asked Naftali.

Naftali didn't answer. Instead he ran over to the sandbox.

"Do you want to help me work on my puzzle?" Avigdor asked me. "I can bring it outside, and we can do it on the picnic table here."

"Sure," I replied.

We worked on the puzzle for nearly an hour. Suddenly I remembered Naftali.

"Oh, no!" I cried. "Where's my brother?"

"Don't worry. I'm sure he's right nearby," Avigdor said.

But I was very worried. I looked all around the park, but I didn't see Naftali.

"Do you know where my little brother is?" I asked the other children.

They just shook their heads.

At that moment, a woman passed by and stopped in front of the sandbox. "Excuse me," she said. "Do you know a little boy who is wearing a yellow shirt and green pants?"

"He's my brother!" I shouted, so excited I jumped up and down. "Where is he?"

The woman pointed to the house next door to the park.

I quickly ran there and saw
Naftali. He was standing
near a sign that said:

Gemach for Lost (and Found) Children

"Is this your brother?"
a nice lady standing near the
sign asked. "Someone found him
on the street and brought him here. We
sent helpers all over the neighborhood to look
for his parents or family."

Just then, a girl walked down the street and
stopped near the nice lady. She said, "I can't
find his family."

A minute later, an older woman returned.
She also said, "I can't find his family."

The nice lady introduced the woman and
girl to me.

"Look who we found! This is Mordechai,
this little boy's brother!"

I took Naftali's hand and thanked the lady

and her helpers for helping Naftali find me. The lady smiled and said, "I'm happy to help. It's a mitzvah to return lost children to their families."

When I returned home, Ima said to me, "Thank you for taking care of Naftali."

"No, Ima, we must thank Hashem, Who takes care of little children, and the *gemach* for lost children," I replied, and then I told her the whole story.

# A Bread Gemach

It was Friday afternoon. The house was almost ready for Shabbos. Ima was mopping the kitchen floor. My older sisters were vacuuming and helping my little brothers and sisters take their baths. Efrayim, Eliezer and I weren't busy, so Ima asked us to set the Shabbos table.

"You bring the cups and I'll bring the plates," Efrayim told me.

Suddenly, we heard a knock. Eliezer ran to the door. Our neighbor, Chaya, a friend of my older sister Zisi, was standing there.

"Can two young Russian Jews spend Shabbos with you?" she asked. "They were supposed to stay at someone else's house. But now they don't have room for them."

"We'll ask our Ima," Eliezer said.

"Ima!" Eliezer screamed. "Can we have two guests from Russia for Shabbos?"

"Of course," Ima replied.

"Of course," Abba also said.

"But Russia is far away and it's almost Shabbos!" Efrayim protested. "How will they make it on time?"

"They're not in Russia now, silly," Abba replied. "They're here in America!"

"Oh," Eliezer said. "But, Ima! What if we don't have enough food?"

"We'll have enough, Eliezer," she said. She took some fish and chicken out of the freezer.

Ima boiled some water and Abba brought in more chairs. But we children also wanted to help. We brought two more plates, cups, knives, forks and spoons to the table.

"Bring pretty napkins, too, in honor of the guests," Efrayim said.

Suddenly, we heard another knock. Chaya was at the door again.

"Mrs. Cohen," Chaya asked, "can two more guests come?"

"Of course!" Ima replied. "I have plenty of fish and meat."

But after Ima closed the door, she remembered that she didn't have enough challah.

Ima called Chaya's mother and told her the problem. Chaya's mother said: "Don't worry. The Levi family has a bread and challah *gemach*."

Efrayim and I ran to the Levi house. It was almost Shabbos. We knocked on the door and, when Mrs. Levi answered, we asked if she had some challah. "We have 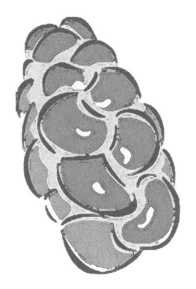 four extra guests for Shabbos!" we explained excitedly.

Mrs. Levi invited us into the kitchen. She opened her freezer and took out three challahs. She put them in a bag and gave it to us. We thanked her and ran home.

We had a wonderful Shabbos. Our guests were very happy. We sang *zemiros* and told many stories. Abba explained the meaning of Shabbos to our guests. *Baruch Hashem*, there was plenty of food and, thanks to Mrs. Levi's bread and challah *gemach*, there was enough challah for everyone!

CHAPTER
4

# A Homework Gemach

We have a basement in our apartment building. It is very large and contains an old table, many old chairs, two wooden beds and some Sukkah boards.

On most days, no one goes there. Only during the summer—when my neighbor Chavi has a day camp there—is it used. Then, when camp is over, my sisters Rina and Zisi help her clean the basement.

One winter day, Zisi said to Rina, "Let's go down to the basement."

"Why?" Rina asked.

"I want to look at it," she explained.

They opened the basement's creaky door and went inside. It was dark and cold. Rina turned on the light.

"I have an idea," Zisi said. "If we clean the chairs and tables, we can play here every day. We can even invite our friends. It'll be fun!"

"We can bring our younger brothers and sisters with us and let Ima rest in the afternoon. We can even do our homework here!" Rina suggested.

Zisi and Rina were very excited and made many plans.

At night, before they went to bed, Zisi said: "I thought of an even better idea. Let's make a *gemach* in the basement — a homework *gemach*! We can invite all of the children in the neighborhood to do their homework in the basement. We can help the younger ones, too!"

The next morning, they jumped out of bed. "Ima," they said, "we would like to open a new *gemach*, right here in our building."

"What kind of a *gemach* — a candy *gemach*?" she said laughing.

"No. A helpful *gemach*. A homework *gemach*!"

"That's a very good idea," she replied. "But our apartment is very small."

"That's no problem, Ima," Zisi said. "We can use the basement. We'll help younger children do their homework. We can even bring toys for the really little ones."

"You are great kids," Ima said with a smile. Then she kissed them.

In the afternoon, they made a big sign and hung it up near the grocery store. It said: *"Homework Gemach. Open every day from 4:30 p.m. to 6:30 p.m. 1435 49th Street."*

HOMEWORK GEMACH
Open every day from
4:30 p.m. to 6:30 p.m.
1435 49th Street

Children came to the homework *gemach* every day. My sisters helped them with their homework while their mothers rested.

One day, a little girl named Sarah Schwartz showed them a note. It said:

*Dear Mrs. Schwartz,*

*Sarah does her homework every day.*

*She is doing very well in school.*

*Morah Roth*

"Thank you so much for helping me!" Sarah told them. "My mother is so happy!"

Zisi and Rina were also happy, because it is a mitzvah to help others. They continue to help kids with their homework to this day!

# CHAPTER 5

# A Bottle Gemach

My baby sister, Penina, loses her bottle at least five times a day. Sometimes three-year-old Miri takes the bottle and drinks from it herself. Sometimes Penina hides it and forgets where she put it.

Penina can't fall asleep without her bottle. If Ima can't find it, she asks us to help her.

We usually find it. But one time we couldn't find the bottle.

My mother had put Penina to bed at seven o'clock. Rina and I were doing our homework.

Ima said: "The baby is sleeping. I am going to visit Mrs. Katz, because she is not feeling well. Can you two keep an eye on things until I get back?"

Soon after she left, Penina suddenly began to cry. Soon her cries turned into screams.

"Give her a bottle," I said.

"Where is it?" Rina asked.

It wasn't on the table.
It wasn't on the bed.
It wasn't in her crib.

"*B-a-t-i!*" Penina cried.

"Penina, where is your bottle?" Rina asked.

"*B-a-t-i,*" she cried again.

"Let's look in the kitchen," Rina suggested.

We searched the kitchen, the living room and the porch. But we couldn't find a single bottle!

Penina began to scream loudly.

Suddenly, I remembered: "Mrs. Turk, our neighbor, has a *gemach* for bottles! I'll go there."

"Please hurry!" Rina said.

I ran to Mrs. Turk's house and knocked on the door.

"Who's there?" Mrs. Turk asked.

"Mordechai Cohen."

"Hi, Mordechai! How can I help you?"

"My baby sister lost her bottle. She is crying and we can't find any other bottles. Do you have any bottles?"

Mrs. Turk laughed. "Our *gemach* is not for

baby bottles. It's for bottles of soda and drinks! Sometimes people forget to buy drinks for Shabbos or for a simcha, and we give them some. But don't worry. Mrs. Lerner has a *gemach* for baby bottles. I'll take you there."

It was eight o'clock at night. But Mrs. Turk put on her coat and took me to Mrs. Lerner's house.

I was glad that she took me. It was dark outside and I was afraid.

We knocked, and Mrs. Lerner answered the door.

"Can I help you?" she asked.

When I told her the problem, she asked me to come choose a bottle. She said I should choose a color that Penina would like.

"Penina likes red bottles," I said. "Thank you so much!"

Mrs. Lerner gave me a red bottle and Mrs. Turk took me home.

When I arrived, I couldn't believe it. Penina was still screaming.

I took the bottle and ran to the kitchen. When I opened the refrigerator to take out some milk, guess what I found behind the milk? Penina's bottle!

So sometimes, I guess, a *gemach* is also good for people who have things in their house but just can't find them!

# A Simcha Gemach

Last year, my sister Ruti got engaged.

We were all so happy! Ima and Ruti shopped for a beautiful white wedding gown for Ruti. Ima bought new clothes for all of us. My older sisters helped choose the flowers. Abba, Ima and Ruti chose the invitations and the wedding hall.

We were all very excited and couldn't wait for the wedding day.

On the day of the wedding, it was very cold outside. Large snowflakes began to fall. Children ran outside to build snowmen. They were very excited to play in the snow.

But my sister Ruti was worried.

"Who will come to my wedding?" she asked. "It's so cold. There are no buses, and the highways are dangerous."

We took a taxi to the wedding hall. Not too many people showed up.

After the *chuppah*, we sat down to eat. Aunt Deena told us that it had stopped snowing.

Soon the *chassan*'s friends came and the music began to play.

Suddenly, a large group of girls entered the hall and began to dance.

"Who are they?" I asked my sister.

"I don't know," she said.

My aunt asked some of the girls, "Are you Ruti's friends?"

"No," they replied. "We are everyone's friends! We live near the hall. When it snows or rains, we come here to dance with the bride and make her happy. We are a simcha *gemach*!"

My whole family smiled at the idea. We were happy someone could make my sister's wedding happier.

# CHAPTER 7

# A Chickpea Gemach

Early Friday morning, the telephone rang. My older sister Zisi answered.

"Really?" she screamed. "I don't believe it! That's so exciting! Mazel tov!"

"Who's on the phone? Who's on the phone?" we all asked excitedly. We knew that something had happened, something good.

But what? We jumped up and down, screaming: "Tell us! Tell us who's on the phone!"

I wanted to ask Abba and Ima what had happened. I knocked on their door, but no one answered.

"Where is Ima? Where is Abba?" I asked.

"Do you want to speak with Mordechai?" I heard Zisi ask over the phone. Then she told me to come to the telephone.

"Abba is on the phone," Zisi said.

I went to the phone, and said, "Hello, Abba. Why aren't you at home? Where are you?"

"I'm in the hospital. Ima had a baby boy! You have a new brother."

We all began to sing and dance. I was the happiest of all because now there would be as many boys as girls in my family!

Later that day, when we returned from school, Abba was in the kitchen. He said: "Everything is ready for Shabbos. But we don't have chickpeas for the Shalom Zachor. What will we do?"

I was sad. Everyone I knew always had chickpeas at a Shalom Zachor.

Suddenly, I remembered Yitzchak Zilber from my class. His mother has an *arbess* (chickpeas) *gemach*. She makes a lot of chickpeas once a month and puts them in the freezer. When someone needs them for a Shalom Zachor, she is always ready.

It was nearly one o'clock. Yitzchak Zilber lives on 60th street, which is far from my house. But we needed chickpeas!

I ran all the way to Yitzchak's house and

even ran up the tall flight of steps leading to his house. Yitzchak opened the door. He was surprised to see me.

"Yitzchak," I said, "can you give me some chickpeas?"

He laughed. He thought that I wanted a snack.

"Yitzchak," I said, "my mother had a baby boy this morning! Now I have another brother!"

"Mazel tov! Mazel tov!" he cried, a big smile on his face.

Yitzchak called his mother. She was in the kitchen.

"Mordechai's mother had a baby boy!" he said.

"Mazel tov! Mazel tov!" she cried.

"He needs chickpeas—lots of them."

Yitzchak's mother went to the freezer and took out a large bag. "This has two pounds of chickpeas," she said. "Is it too heavy?"

"No," I replied. "Thank you very much. Abba will be very happy."

That night, after the Shabbos meal, all our neighbors came to our Shalom Zachor.

"The chickpeas are delicious," everyone said.

"They have a special flavor," my father said. "The flavor of *chessed*!"

# A Shabbos Gemach

It was Shabbos. Eliezer's seat was empty. So was Abba's. I made Kiddush. Ima told us stories.

Where was Eliezer? Where was Abba? They were in the hospital. Eliezer did not feel well.

"What will Abba eat in the hospital?"

Efrayim asked. "Where will he sleep?"

"Does he have wine for Kiddush?" Rina asked. "Does he have challah? Will he sing *zemiros* by himself? Is there a shul in the hospital?"

Abba and Eliezer returned home after Shabbos. Abba said: "Eliezer feels better. His stomach doesn't hurt anymore. He can even go to school tomorrow."

"What was wrong with him?" Ima asked. "Did he have appendicitis?"

"No," Abba said. "Eliezer, tell Ima what happened."

Eliezer began his story …

When we got to the hospital, the doctor asked me what hurt. I pointed to my stomach. The doctor examined me and gave me some medicine. I fell asleep. When I woke up, I felt better. It was already Shabbos and I wanted to go home.

But the doctor said, "I must check you again." Then he asked, "Did you eat too much ice cream?"

"I didn't eat ice cream," I explained. "I ate green apples."

"How many did you eat?" he asked.

"My friend Menachem and I wanted to see who could eat more green apples. Menachem ate only four. I won. I ate six."

The doctor laughed. Then he said, "You aren't sick. I have to send you home."

Abba was worried. It was already Shabbos and our house was far away from the hospital.

Suddenly, a man with a beard came over to him and said: "My name is Tuvia. Please come to our house for Shabbos. We live near the hospital. Every Shabbos I come to the hospital to see if people need a place to stay. We have a special room in our house for guests. We have a Shabbos *gemach*."

We said good-bye to the doctors and the nurses. The doctor smiled at me and said: "Next time, don't eat so many green apples! Have a good Shabbos!"

We went home with Tuvia. His children met him at the door.

"Abba, did you bring us a guest for Shabbos?" they asked.

"Two," he replied. "Please show them their room, and bring them some cake and tea. But don't give Eliezer any green apples!" he said with a big smile.

Tuvia's wife had already lit the Shabbos candles, so we went to shul. Shabbos in their house was so much fun! We sang *zemiros*, told stories, studied the *parsha* and ate really delicious food. On Motzai Shabbos, Tuvia even gave us money for a taxi. And here we are!

Everyone laughed. Ima told Eliezer that he could have a banana, but no more green apples!

Abba then said: "Tuvia's house is just like the tent of Avraham Avinu. Guests are always welcome!"

# A Glasses Gemach

My brother Efrayim wears very thick glasses. Without his glasses, he can't see the blackboard. He can't see his Rebbi's face. He can't even see what's on his sandwich!

Everyone loves Efrayim because he is so kind and friendly. He is a good student, too.

One day, Efrayim ran into his class. He

was very excited because there was a Chumash test and he loves Chumash. He even loves Chumash tests!

Just then, Asher ran out of the classroom and—boom!—Asher and Efrayim ran right into each other. Efrayim's glasses fell down and broke. There was a cut on Asher's face. The Rebbi washed Asher's face and told both boys to sit down. "You can take the test tomorrow, Efrayim. Your mother will get you new glasses this afternoon."

"But I love Chumash and I want to learn today!" Efrayim cried. "I want my glasses now!"

Suddenly, Menachem had an idea. He said, "My neighbor, Mr. Weiner, has a glasses *gemach.* He lives one block away from school.

His wife is at home. Perhaps he has glasses for Efrayim. Can I take Efrayim to the *gemach* now?"

"Yes," the Rebbi said. "What a great idea, Menachem!"

Menachem took Efrayim's hand and led him to the *gemach*.

Mrs. Weiner was home. She had Efrayim try on a bunch of glasses to see which worked best for him. When he had picked one out,

 Mrs. Weiner said: "You can return these when your mother buys you new ones."

The glasses looked very funny. They were very big and had black frames. They slipped down Efrayim's nose. He laughed and his friends laughed. Even the Rebbi laughed.

But Efrayim was very happy. "Now I can see the blackboard. Now I can see the Rebbi. Now I can read the precious words of the Chumash," he said.

# CHAPTER 10

# A Family Gemach

Miri stood near Ima and cried, "Ima, I can't reach my doll. Can you get it for me?"

"I'm busy now," Ima said. "Ask Zisi to bring you the doll."

"Zisi's busy, too. She's doing her homework."

"So ask Rina."

"I already asked her! She's talking on the

telephone. She said, 'Not now.' "

"Ask Mordechai."

Miri went to the porch. I was there. I was talking to my best friend Shmuel.

"Look at that new building," Shmuel said. "No one lives there yet."

"It has four floors and a lot of apartments. I hope that a lot of kids move in," I replied.

"Mordechai, please get me my doll. It's on the top shelf," Miri cried.

"When new people move in, we can help the little kids with their homework," I continued, ignoring Miri.

"I can walk the little ones to school in the morning," Shmuel added.

"Mordechai, I want my doll. *P-l-e-a-s-e.*"

"I'll help them shop and I'll ask Ima to

bake them cakes for Shabbos."

Miri began to cry.

"Why is your sister crying?" Shmuel asked.

"She always cries," I replied, looking at Miri and shaking my head. "Let's go inside. I don't like crying!"

Suddenly, Ima came out to the porch. "Miri, why are you crying?" she asked.

"I want my doll. It's on the top shelf."

"Mordechai, why didn't you give her the doll?"

"She didn't ask me for it."

"That's not true," Shmuel said. "She asked you for the doll. You just didn't hear her."

Ima went with Miri to the children's room and took down the doll.

"Here, Miri. Sit down and play," she said.

Miri stopped crying.

Shmuel and I came into the room.

Suddenly, Shmuel said: "You know my little brother Avraham Yosef? Today he wanted to come with me to your house. I told him: 'You can't come. I don't need a shadow.' Now I'm sorry. When I saw Miri crying, I remembered my brother. I'm sorry that I was mean to him. I think that we should help our own families, not only people in new buildings."

"You're right!" I happily said. "Let's open a *gemach*! We can call it a 'family *gemach*.' We will help all our brothers, sisters and parents."

"That's a great idea!" Shmuel said. "I'll have a family *gemach* in my house. You can

open one in your house. Everyone in the world can open this kind of *gemach*."

"Let's put a sign up that says: 'A *Gemach* In Every House!'"

"What a smart idea!" I said. "The rules of the *gemach* will be:

- When Ima calls, come immediately.
- When little sisters cry, ask them what they want.
- Don't fight.
- Help your brothers and sisters with their homework."

Shmuel added: "Let's ask the newspapers to announce:

*'There is a new gemach in town—*
*A family gemach!*
*Hours: All day and all night.*
*Place: Everywhere!'*"

THE CHILDREN'S LEARNING SERIES

STORIES ABOUT YOU AND ME

# HAND IN HAND

BY MENUCHA FUCHS · ILLUSTRATED BY YONI

# The Mystery Package

I put my hand into the mailbox and felt all around. "A letter!" I said happily.

I check the mailbox every day when I come home from school. So do my brothers and sisters. Today I got lucky—I was first at the mailbox. But what I held was not an ordinary letter. It was a card. On it, in big red letters, was written "Large Package." I was so excited. I ran upstairs as fast as I could.

"Look! Look what we got in the mail," I shouted to my mother as I waved the card around.

My mother took the card and read it carefully. Then she looked at her watch and said: "Mordechai, the post office is closed now. But you can go tomorrow and bring the package home. Okay?"

"All right, Ima," I replied and added in an important voice, "you can trust me — I'll take good care of the package."

I could hardly wait for the next day to arrive. The post office had written: "Large Package." But who could have sent us a large package? Could we have won a prize? Or could someone have sent us some books? I couldn't figure it out.

Finally, school ended—it was time to go and pick up the

package. On my way to the post office, I stopped at my friend Avner Katz's house to see if he wanted to come with me. I wondered what he would say about the mysterious package.

Avner was really excited. Of course he wanted to be the first to see my large package.

"Don't you have an aunt, grandmother or someone in another state?" he asked.

"Why do you ask?"

"Because we once received a huge package

from California. It was from our grandmother. She filled it with toys and clothes for all of us."

I tried very hard to remember any cousins in California. Suddenly, I remembered a cousin of my mother's who lived somewhere far away — maybe California. I have never met her, but my mother sends her a pretty Rosh Hashanah card every year. Once they even spoke on the phone.

"That's it!" I cried. "I'm sure that she sent the package. Hurray — a huge package filled with clothes and toys for all of us!"

"Should we ask Shalom to help us?" asked Avner. "A big package can be very heavy."

When we reached his house, Shalom came out to greet us. He was eager to help and even suggested that his older brothers come along, too.

Of course, I agreed. Shimon, Shalom's

oldest brother, said that we should bring his wagon, too.

Five minutes later, we arrived at the post office pulling the heavy wagon behind us.

"Please wait outside. It'll look funny if we all go in together," I explained.

As I entered, I was so excited that I could feel my heart beating rapidly. I gave the card to the clerk. He went to the back room and, when he came out, he handed me a small, thin package—as big as two envelopes—no more.

"What's this?" I asked in surprise.

"It's yours," answered the clerk.

"But, but … I don't understand," I said, looking at the small package. "The card said 'Large Package.'"

"That's right," answered the smiling clerk. "It was too big to fit into your mailbox."

I didn't answer. I went outside to my friends. They looked at me and then stared at the small package in my hand. Then they looked at me again.

Suddenly, they all began to laugh. I laughed, too. We laughed and laughed as we and our big empty wagon slowly returned home.

# The Strange Gift

"Please be a little bit quieter!" my mother said to us.

We were being very noisy. Of course, it's very hard for four girls to talk quietly. But it was true that this time we really were too noisy.

"Ima," I apologized, "we were just having

fun now that vacation is here!"

My mother didn't see it our way.

"You must learn to speak quietly. It's not nice to speak so loud. If you yell when you are on vacation, you will speak like that all the time. If you shout when you're at home, you will also speak too loudly outside."

We knew that my mother was right. Only yesterday we had sat in front of the house talking. My mother had overheard everything from our balcony! When she told us, we were so embarrassed! If she had heard us, then maybe our neighbors had, too. Did we want everyone to know all about our class, our friends and our plans?

Even though we knew that my mother was right, we kept forgetting. The next time we met, we talked and laughed as loudly as ever.

A few days later we went to Michal's house.

We sat on her large balcony and—again, without really realizing it—we spoke very loudly.

"Tomorrow is Esther's birthday," Michal suddenly remembered. "Let's buy her a gift."

"Of course," I agreed. "But should we each buy her a gift or should we chip in together?"

After much discussion, we decided to buy one special gift from all of us. But the next problem was what we should buy.

"We can't buy her a pen—she already has six," said Bat-Sheva.

"At least!" laughed Yocheved. "Let's buy

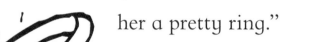 her a pretty ring."

"No," I said. "Esther doesn't like rings because you have to take them off every time you wash your hands. She loses them all the time. I know! Let's get her some pretty flowers from Mrs. Black's flower store. We can include a nice letter that we could decorate."

"Great!" agreed Michal and Yocheved.

"Flowers are always nice," added Bat-Sheva. "We can send them from the flower store."

"What's Esther's address?" asked Michal. "I know where she lives but I always forget her address."

Everyone looked at me. I knew the address, and in my loudest, clearest voice said, "Esther Weiss, 1444 – 47th Street."

It was late. We quickly decided how much money we could each afford. Then we chose a time to meet to pick out the flowers.

Esther received two bouquets of flowers for

her birthday. One was small but very pretty.

The other was only one half-dead flower, with a strange note attached.

Esther called to tell us she was thrilled with our flowers and the nice card we had included. But who had sent her that other flower?

Esther ran over to my house to show us the strange note. It said:

*To Esther Weiss,*

*Happy Birthday from Michal's neighbor, who was sick and was not able to rest because of your birthday ….*

"Why did I receive this? How did this person know it was my birthday, and my name and address?" she asked.

We knew. We understood. Because we were so inconsiderate, a sick person was not able to get her much needed rest.

This was something serious. Something *very* serious. Boy, did we learn to speak more quietly after that!

# CHAPTER 3

ZISI'S STORY

# All For Nothing?

I tried to remember the address she had given me over the telephone, but I couldn't. *Why, oh why, hadn't I written it down?*

I buttoned the last button on my coat on this cold, rainy day in February. My head hurt. "What a day," I said to myself as I thought about how it had all begun.

A woman named Mrs. Rubin had phoned me and said, "I am the mother of two sweet little girls, Shaindel and Chaya. We live near 13th Avenue. Could you come over and baby-sit for my daughters?"

I didn't know Mrs. Rubin. I asked her how she had gotten my name.

"I got it from your classmate, Hadassah Miller. She said so many nice things about you that I decided to ask you to baby-sit."

My mother and I agreed that I really had too much to do at home. I also wanted to study. But I was flattered by the thought that Mrs. Rubin had chosen me from all my friends. I had never baby-sat before for anyone except my family. But I agreed.

Mrs. Rubin told me the address. I thought it would be easy to remember. I was sure I would remember. But I was wrong.

Now the strong wind blew through the empty, wet street. I was the only one outside. Even the black cat who had been following me now ran inside, away from the rain. I looked at the strange street. I couldn't remember the address. Was it 1325 – 53rd Street or 1353 – 53rd Street or 1353 – 54th Street? I was sure there was a 53 in there somewhere but who could I ask? The street was empty.

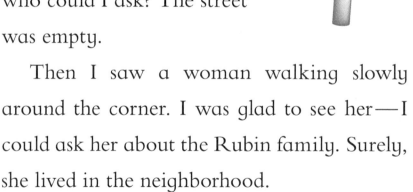

Then I saw a woman walking slowly around the corner. I was glad to see her—I could ask her about the Rubin family. Surely, she lived in the neighborhood.

*I hope she knows*, I thought. *I'm already twenty*

*minutes late. I'm so ashamed! What will Mrs. Rubin think of me now!*

"Excuse me," I said to the woman. She looked surprised, but happy to see me.

"You will help me, won't you?" she asked. At first I didn't understand.

"I am lost. I cannot find my house. Please help me," she asked again, hopefully.

I looked at her face. She looked tired and sad.

"I have been walking around in the wind and rain for more than an hour. I forgot where I live," she said in a combination of English and Yiddish.

*How interesting!* I thought. *I forgot and she forgot. Only someone who forgot would walk around outside in this weather! But how can I find out where she lives? How can I help her? How could a person forget where she lives?*

The old woman continued to tell me about herself, her grandchildren and her great-grandchildren. Standing there in the rain, she even took out pictures to show me! She continued to talk and it was getting later and colder. I thought about poor Mrs. Rubin. What would she think of me now?

"Can I look into your purse?" I asked.

"What? Why do you want my purse?" she asked, holding it close to her heart. She must have

thought I wanted to steal it, *chas v'shalom.*

"Perhaps I can find your address in your purse," I explained slowly.

She finally understood. She gave me her purse and I saw a card that said, "Bella Stern, 1733 – 47th Street."

"No problem," I said happily. "I can take you home now. You live on my street!"

Then I remembered Mrs. Rubin. How could I go home when Mrs. Rubin was waiting for me? She would be angry. My mother would also be angry. But I decided it was more important to help Mrs. Stern get home.

A bus came quickly. It was empty.

"I thank Hashem that you found me," Mrs. Stern repeated the whole way home. "My head hurt and my feet would not move anymore. I was afraid that I would never get home!"

We got off the bus. I held her hand as the wind pushed against us. We were so happy to reach her house! Her husband opened the door and smiled when he saw us.

"I was so worried," he exclaimed. "My wife never goes out alone! The only place she goes alone is to the store. But today she went out and did not return. Thank you very, very much for your help."

When I got home, freezing and wet, my sister Rina told me in an important voice, "Mrs. Rubin called!"

"She did?" I asked quickly. "When?"

"Before," Rina laughed.

"What did she say?" I asked.

I was afraid to hear the answer.

"She said that she is sorry, but in such bad weather she can't go out, and you don't have to baby-sit."

I couldn't believe what I had heard!

"Oh, Zisi! It's too bad you went out in this bad weather for nothing," Rina said sadly.

I smiled and I told Rina the whole story.

My trip was definitely not for nothing!

# True Friends

Suddenly, I saw Kayla pass by. She was with Brachy!

"Where are you going?" I asked. The answer didn't really matter to me. I just wanted them to know that I saw them.

"We're just going outside," they both

answered, looking back at me.

I didn't ask any more questions. I went into my house and slammed the door behind me. I didn't bother to open it again. Even if I had opened the door, I wouldn't have seen them. They had left me behind.

Kayla and I had always been best friends. We were always together — at home, at school, everywhere. We even slept at each other's houses. We were sure we would always be best friends — just the two of us.

But one day everything changed. Ruthie, a new girl from Russia, joined our class. I liked Ruthie as soon as I saw her. In fact, the whole class liked her. From the very beginning, she joined in all of our games.

The next day, I was happy to see Ruthie return my smile. She asked to play with me during recess and I completely forgot about

Kayla. We walked and talked nonstop until the bell rang. I was in my seat when Kayla entered and looked at me angrily.

"Kayla," I said, "do you have the geography book?"

She didn't answer me.

"Why won't you answer me?" I asked again.

"Why don't you ask Ruthie?" she said with a tear in her eye.

At first, I felt bad. Perhaps I shouldn't be Ruthie's friend. Then I thought, *I didn't do anything wrong! Kayla knows that. Anyway, why can't I be friends with both of them?*

The next break came and Kayla seemed okay. We played ball together. But the next day during recess, I played with

Ruthie again. We walked around the school building and talked about our class. Ruthie told me about her old class in Russia and then in Tel Aviv. I listened with interest.

A few days later, Ruthie came to visit me at home. I was so happy that I forgot about Kayla, who was waiting for me at her house. We sat outside to the porch. We talked and laughed. I was telling Kayla's joke to Ruthie about the donkey that began to moo like a cow when Kayla saw  us. She was on her way to the store. She pretended not to see us. We told more jokes until Ruthie jumped up and said, "Oh! I'm late! I forgot that I have an art class today."

*Ruthie is so nice,* I thought as I walked with her to the corner. *But what should I do about*

*Kayla?* Why is she so upset that I have another friend? Next time, should I ask Kayla to join us? No, I can't. Ruthie wants to be *my* friend. I can't ask Kayla to join.

I didn't know how to make everyone happy. Should I stop being Kayla's friend? Could I be friends with both girls—sometimes with one and sometimes with the other?

Sometimes Ruthie played with me. Sometimes she played with Racheli, Naomi, Miriam or Sara. I was happy that Kayla was still my friend. I played with her when I wasn't with Ruthie. But I still didn't understand why Kayla became so upset every time I was with Ruthie.

Finally, when I saw Kayla with her new friend, Brachy, I kind of understood how Kayla felt when she saw me with Ruthie. I felt so alone then, especially when Ruthie didn't come visit me and I was by myself. I would open the front door to go outside and see Kayla and Brachy running down the block. True, sometimes Kayla also played with me in the afternoon. But sometimes I wanted to play with Kayla when she was with Brachy. I didn't think they wanted me to join them.

I was confused. Kayla was my best friend. Was it wrong for her to play with other girls? Was it wrong for *me* to play with other girls? Can't someone have other friends? That's what I thought when Ruthie came to play with me ....

I decided to speak to Kayla about it.

Kayla sighed. "You know, Rina, I used to wish that you would include me when you were playing with Ruthie—that we could all play together. But when I saw that you didn't understand, I decided that it was time for me to find some new friends also. But the truth is I miss being your best friend."

"I'm sorry," I said as I gave Kayla a great big hug.

Now, when Ruthie comes, she comes to play with *both* of us—Kayla and me. And when Brachy comes, all three of us play together, too.

Now everyone knows that it is impossible to come between Kayla and me! We are truly the best of friends!

# Good Neighbors

You probably don't know her. Moshe, Tzvi and I didn't know her either until we heard the following story.

It all began one afternoon. We came home from school a little late. Before we even got off the school bus, we saw the huge truck.

"New neighbors!" shouted Tzvi happily.

"Which apartment will they live in?" asked Moshe.

We watched while the big, strong moving men carried in the refrigerator and furniture.

"We can't wait around for too long," said Tzvi. "My mother wants me home for dinner."

"My mother also doesn't like it when I get home late from school," I added.

We pulled ourselves away from the excitement and hurried home.

"Ima! Ima!" I shouted as I ran into the apartment. "A new neighbor is moving into our building. I saw the truck!"

"I know, Efrayim," my mother answered.

"I wanted to tell you that someone is moving into the apartment downstairs."

"Great!" I shouted happily.

The apartment below us had been empty for months. I was hoping that a family with a boy my age would move in. We could be friends and walk to school together every day.

"Who will live in the apartment?" I asked, hoping to hear the answer I was waiting for.

"A nice woman," my mother replied with a smile.

"A woman?" I asked, disappointed.

"Yes, a lovely old lady who lives by herself," my mother answered. She didn't see the disappointed look in my eyes.

Boy, was I upset! I thought about Moshe and Tzvi, who live in the same building. I was jealous. I wanted a friend in my building, too!

I didn't see the new neighbor that day or the next day. Each day, as I passed her door, I would listen for some noise. But all was quiet.

Three days passed. Then, finally, I saw her one afternoon as I came home from school. She was taking out the garbage. Her arms were full and she couldn't close her door. She didn't see me. I went up to her to say hello. She replied in a funny accent.

"Can I help you?" I asked her. I took the bags and boxes from her and threw them out in the garbage. When I finished, I went back to my house with a funny feeling.

"What happened, Efrayim?" my mother asked when she saw my face.

"Ima! Ima! I met her!"

"Who?" she asked.

"The new neighbor!" I replied. "Why didn't we help her move in? She is all alone and has to do everything by herself."

"I'm happy that you care so much, but don't worry," my mother said. "I already know our new neighbor, Mrs. Schwartz, well. Every day, when you go to school, I go down to help her."

My mother smiled. "It's good that you want to help her. I'm sure that will make her happy. I'll tell her tomorrow morning. In the afternoon, you can go with your friends to help."

When I came by with my friends Moshe and Tzvi in the afternoon, Mrs. Schwartz was waiting for us. But she was a little shy. She didn't know us yet.

It was very difficult for Mrs. Schwartz to manage in her new apartment. She told us she didn't know where to begin!

"I think," said Moshe, "that a plan will help us finish more quickly. When we moved into our new apartment, my mother sat down in the middle of the room full of boxes and wrote a long list of jobs. Each of us wrote down his name next to the jobs he could do."

"That's a great idea," said Tzvi. "I'll get some paper and we can make our list."

"You are wonderful children," said Mrs. Schwartz.

• • •

The neighbors in the building were all very kind. Every day a different neighbor brought a hot meal. One of them brought a delicious cake for Shabbos. We invited our new neighbor for Shabbos meals but she didn't want to come. My mother understood. She said that Mrs. Schwartz might feel a little shy. But we couldn't understand how she could want to be alone on Shabbos.

"What about *zemiros*?" we asked.

The minute we asked the question, we already knew the answer. Moshe and Tzvi immediately agreed. As soon as we finished our Shabbos meals, we all met outside her door. When she opened the door for us, she wished us "Good Shabbos."

"Have you come to visit me today?" she asked with a smile. "Please come in."

The boxes were all gone. The apartment was now clean and neat.

"We came to sing *zemiros* for you," we told her shyly.

"To sing? I love singing. My children used to sing …."

"You have children?" we asked in surprise.

"Yes, I have two. But they are not young children. They have their own families. They live in Russia, where I used to live. I hope they will come to live here soon," she said sadly.

We began to sing as nicely as we could. We sang many *zemiros*. Mrs. Schwartz smiled happily. She was so happy she even cried a little. We were also very happy. (But we didn't cry!)

• • •

One day, when we came to visit her, there was a surprise. Three boys our age stood there. We knew they didn't live in our neighborhood.

"Daniel, Yanky, Shaul—look who is here! These are the boys I told you about," she said to them.

To us, she said, "Please meet my grandsons. They are nine, ten and eleven years old. They just came from Russia to live in America. Isn't this a great surprise?"

Now we have new friends. Their parents found an apartment near our building. The boys come often to visit their grandmother. At first, they didn't speak English very well. But now they speak almost perfectly!

Do you remember how sad I was when the new neighbor—not a family—moved in? Now I am so happy! I have a nice, new neighbor, I was able to do many mitzvos, and now ... I have three new friends!

CHAPTER
6
MORDECHAI'S STORY

# Our Mitzvah Muscles

We want to be painters when we grow up!

"Painters?" you ask?

Read this story and you will understand.

It all began with the writing on the wall. One day, as we walked up the stairs in our building, we saw children's scribbles on the walls.

"What a pity," said Chaim sadly. "The walls were always so nice and clean. Look at them now! Who did this?"

"Does it matter?" I asked. "It could be any of the children in the building. But, *oy*, what a mess!"

When I reached our home, I saw that I was not the only one who was upset. My mother said that we should call a painter. Father agreed to call David. He's the painter we use whenever we paint our home. He is an excellent painter. He works hard to support his family.

David had another job in the morning, but he agreed to paint our building in the afternoon. My friend Chaim and I were happy. That meant we could watch him work.

Chaim and I stood near the door and watched David bring in an old ladder, paint and two brushes. We watched him climb to the very top of the ladder. Then, all of a sudden, he fell!

We shouted for help. We were so scared to see our strong friend David on the floor and in pain. Neighbors quickly came to help. My father helped David stand up slowly and took him to the hospital in his car.

"Poor David! I hope he will be okay," my mother said. Chaim's mother agreed.

Soon the hall was empty again. Chaim and I stood alone. We looked at David's ladder, paint and brushes.

"I have an idea!" shouted Chaim. "We can finish the job ourselves!"

I wasn't sure about the idea. But Chaim

said, "Come on! It's not so hard to paint!"

We began to work. At first, it was fun to spread the paint over the walls. It was nice to make all the marks on the walls go away. But the work became harder and harder. Our arms hurt. Our legs hurt. Soon we were so tired that we wanted to give up.

We stopped to look at what we had done so far. How clean the walls looked! True, we were tired. But when we saw what we had done, it made all the hard work seem worth it.

So we decided to continue. We moved up to the second floor, and the time just flew by.

"Wonderful!" said Chaim's father when he and my father came to check on us. They were surprised to see how much we had painted.

"Chaim and Mordechai—you are as good as real painters!" my father added.

"Thank you!" I said. "But how is David feeling?"

"David must rest," Chaim's father explained. "He broke his leg, and he hurt his head. He won't to able to do any painting for a while."

We asked if David could be paid for the painting job even though we finished it for him. My father agreed.

We worked quickly. When we finished, we went to visit David. My father gave him the money. He was happy to see us and so surprised to receive the money.

"Thank you so much for being my helpers today!" he said as he smiled at us.

When we came home, we were very tired

and covered with paint. We were more tired than we had ever been before.

But we also felt something special. It was the feeling you got from doing a mitzvah with every muscle in your body!

# CHAPTER 7

EFRAYIM'S STORY

# Partners

"How many Rebbe pictures do you have?" my neighbor Shloimy asked me.

"I have ten at home," I answered. "But I only have three pictures in my pocket."

"Can I see them?" Shloimy asked.

I took them out and gave them to Shloimy.

Shloimy looked at each one carefully, and then said, smiling a big smile, "I have lots more pictures than you do!"

"Could I come and see your pictures?" I asked shyly. Shloimy is two years older than I am and I wasn't sure if he would let me come to his house.

"Why not? Come over this afternoon and I'll show you my album."

I was happy to go. A big shiny album with many pictures of Rebbes sat on his desk.

"How did you get so many?" I asked.

"I try to get as many pictures as I can. On

Shabbos, I go to a Tehillim group, and every night I study in a special learning group. I try to get pictures in many different ways."

I looked again at all the pictures in the album. Some names were new to me. There were some Rebbes whose names I knew, but whose faces I hadn't known.

"So what do you think of my album?" asked Shloimy proudly.

"It's great!" I answered.

"Would you like to be my partner?" Shloimy asked.

"Partner?" I was surprised. "You have so many more pictures than I do. Why would you want me for a partner?"

"Why not? It's no big deal," answered Shloimy.

We both ran to my house and got my pictures, and we put them into Shloimy's special album.

I started going to the learning group every night and to the Shabbos Tehillim group. I really liked going, and whenever I went I got more Rebbe pictures. When Shloimy saw how many pictures I had collected, he smiled and told me I was doing a great job.

At first, Shloimy and I met on Shabbos and I gave him the pictures then. After a while, though, he spent more time learning, so we didn't meet as often. He said I could go to his house and ask his mother for the album whenever I wanted, but I didn't. I was busy getting more and more pictures all the time.

I didn't go to Shloimy's house for a few weeks. Then, one day, as I was coming home from school, I  saw a big moving truck outside our building.

"Where have I seen that furniture before?" I tried to remember. When the truck drove away, I remembered. It was Shloimy's furniture! I ran to his house and knocked on the door. No one answered.

I knocked harder and harder because I was angry, but the door didn't open.

Why didn't Shloimy tell me he was moving?

Suddenly, I knew why he wanted to be partners. He wanted to take my pictures for his album!

The next day, I went into Shloimy's class. I thought his classmates would probably be interested in hearing my story.

"Hey, Asher, listen to this," I called to a boy I knew from my block.

Asher looked at me. The other boys in the classroom also turned to me.

"Do you remember Shloimy?" I asked.

They looked at me as if I were crazy. Shloimy had only left yesterday—how could they have forgotten him?

"His family had to leave suddenly for some reason," said Asher.

"Yes, I know his reason. He wanted all the pictures from—"

Zev stopped me in the middle of my sentence. Zev was Shloimy's best friend.

"Oh, Efrayim! I'm so happy you're here! Before Shloimy left, he asked me to give you the album. He said that you should continue to get more pictures and put them in the album. He'll also get more pictures. Can you come over this afternoon to pick it up?"

I didn't answer. I thought about what I had been about to say.

"So … what were you saying?" asked Zev.

"Uh … nothing, really." I was ashamed. But I decided that what had happened was actually a good story with an important lesson, so I told the boys the story I am telling you now.

# CHAPTER 1

# Telling Jokes

Eliezer's friend Daniel is so funny. Daniel always tells jokes. Sometimes he tells jokes that he has heard from other people. Those jokes are funny. But Daniel's funniest jokes are the ones that he makes up on the spot. Daniel jokes always get a laugh! Eliezer and his friends all love Daniel's jokes.

There is only one problem. Daniel does not know when to stop telling jokes. He even tells jokes during class. This makes his teacher, Rabbi Hertz, very upset.

"Daniel," Rabbi Hertz explained one day after class, "please don't tell jokes during class! You have a great sense of humor. But when you tell jokes, I can't teach. Your friends can't learn. They are too busy laughing. Please save your jokes for recess or after school."

Daniel tried to listen to his teacher's advice. He tried not to tell jokes during class. But it was too hard for him not to tell jokes. He likes making people laugh.

Last Monday, during the Chumash class, Rabbi Hertz was teaching about Yaakov Avinu.

"Who can tell me who Yaakov was?"

Rabbi Hertz asked.

Before anybody could answer, Daniel started speaking.

"That's easy," Daniel said. "Yaakov lives next door to me. He is six years old and loves playing with his red car."

All the boys in the class started laughing. Eliezer couldn't stop laughing. But Rabbi Hertz was not laughing.

"Daniel," Rabbi Hertz said, "we are learning Torah. Now is not the time for telling jokes!"

Daniel was sad. He didn't want to upset Rabbi Hertz. But everybody else enjoyed his jokes so much! He liked to see his friends happy! Daniel didn't know what to do.

Eliezer felt sorry for Daniel. He didn't want teachers to be upset at Daniel all the time.

"I don't know what to do, Eliezer," Daniel said. "I don't want to make Rabbi Hertz upset. I don't want to stop my friends from learning. But I can't stop telling jokes!"

Eliezer thought about how he could help his friend. Finally, he came up with a good idea.

The next morning, before school began, Eliezer spoke to a few of his friends.

"Listen," Eliezer said. "I think we shouldn't laugh at the jokes Daniel tells during class."

"Why?" asked Avi. "We like Daniel's jokes!"

"I like them, too," Eliezer answered. "But if we don't laugh, maybe Daniel will stop telling jokes. Then Rabbi Hertz won't be angry and Daniel won't get in trouble."

"Okay," his friends agreed. "We'll only laugh at his jokes when we aren't in class."

Soon after class began, Daniel told his first joke. Nobody in the class laughed. Daniel wondered what happened and tried to tell another joke. Again, nobody laughed.

*If nobody likes my jokes, I guess I'll just stop telling them*, Daniel thought.

During recess, Eliezer and his friends laughed about the jokes Daniel had told earlier.

*Oh*, thought Daniel. *They will only laugh at my jokes outside of class! I understand. From now on, I'll only tell jokes during recess.*

"Mazel tov," Eliezer told Daniel the next day. "I told you that you could do it!"

Daniel smiled and said, "Yes, I stopped telling jokes during class. Now the teachers won't always be mad at me. I couldn't have done it without the help of my friends. Thank you."

"And," he continued, "that reminds me of a funny joke ...."

Daniel and Eliezer looked at each other and laughed.

# CHAPTER 2

# The Pajama Problem

"What's sticking out from under your clothes?" Eliezer's friend Benji asked him.

Eliezer looked down. He turned red.

"Oh, no!" Eliezer said. "I can't believe it! I forgot to take off my pajama pants!"

"That's so funny! I can't believe it!" giggled Benji.

Soon more boys noticed. They all started laughing.

Eliezer was not laughing. He didn't think it was funny. He was embarrassed that he had forgotten to take off his pajamas. And he was upset that Benji was laughing at him. He thought Benji was his friend!

*Seven-year-old boys shouldn't forget things like this*, Eliezer thought. *I hope nobody else notices my mistake.* Eliezer tucked his pajamas carefully under his clothing.

"Ima," Eliezer said when he got home, "I did the silliest thing today! I forgot to take off my pajama pants before I got dressed. I don't know how I could have done that. I want to make sure I never ever forget again."

"Don't worry about it, Eliezer," said Ima. "I'm sure you will think of a way to help you remember from now on."

Eliezer thought and thought. Finally, he said, "Maybe, Ima, you could wake me up a little earlier in the morning. Then I wouldn't have to rush as much!"

"Good idea, Eliezer," said Ima. "I'll wake you when I get up in the morning."

The next day, Ima woke Eliezer early. He happily jumped out of bed and started getting ready for school.

Of course, he remembered to change out of his pajama pants. That was the reason he had gotten up so early! Eliezer dressed and ate his breakfast. He kissed his Ima good-bye and left for school.

Soon he met his friend Benji.

"Guess what, Benji!" said Eliezer. "I remembered to take off my pajama pants today."

"Great!" said Benji, with a smile. "But … what's that sticking out from under your shirt? Did you leave on your pajama *shirt*?"

Eliezer was quiet. His face turned red and he thought he was about to cry. Benji was sorry that his friend was upset. He didn't know what to say. He didn't want Eliezer to cry. Benji said, "Don't worry, Eliezer! You'll remember tomorrow!"

Suddenly, Eliezer smiled a big smile. It lit up his whole face.

"Eliezer," Benji asked, "why are you smiling?"

"It's very simple," said Eliezer. "I'm happy. If I remembered to take off my pajama pants today, I can remember to take off my pajama shirt tomorrow. I know I can do anything I set my mind to do!"

"Good for you," said Benji. "I'm sure you will remember! And I'm sorry I laughed at you. It was the wrong thing to do. I didn't mean to upset you."

Eliezer smiled. Benji was his friend, after all! But sometimes things are just funny and even your friends can't help but laugh!

Sure enough, the next day Eliezer remembered to take off both his pajama pants and shirt. And he never made that mistake again!

# CHAPTER 3

# Backpacks

Every morning, when it is time to go to school, Eliezer puts his backpack on his back. It is always heavy, and Eliezer always says, "Ugh, this is so heavy. Are there really only books in my backpack? I feel like I am carrying a big tree!"

When school is over, Eliezer puts his

backpack on his back again. It is still very heavy.

One day, while Eliezer was walking to the bus stop with his friends, he had a great idea.

"Five of us take the same bus every day," Eliezer told his friends. "We live near each other. We each carry a heavy backpack. Let's take turns carrying the backpacks. Each day a different one of us can carry them. That way, nobody will have to carry a backpack every day. Today Moshe can carry all of our backpacks. Tomorrow Eli can carry them. We can switch off every day."

Eliezer's friends liked his idea. They agreed to try it.

They each gave their backpack to Moshe.

He picked them up one at a time. He started to walk. It was not easy, but Moshe did it. He was able to carry all of their backpacks. He put Levi's green backpack on one shoulder and Shimon's purple backpack on his other shoulder. He grabbed Eliezer's black backpack in one hand and Eli's blue backpack in the other. Moshe walked slowly because the bags were very heavy.

Levi, Shimon, Eliezer and Eli were happy that they did not have to carry their heavy backpacks. They hardly noticed how unhappy

Moshe looked.

"This was a great idea, Eliezer!" said Levi.

The next day, Eli carried all the backpacks. Eli is small. He is not as strong as Moshe. It was hard for him to carry all the bags. But none of the other boys helped him. They were just happy that they didn't have to carry their backpacks.

On Friday, it was Eliezer's turn to carry all the backpacks.

*Oh, no,* Eliezer thought. *How am I going to carry all those heavy backpacks?*

Eli handed him his blue backpack. Eliezer put it on his right shoulder.

"Why is it so heavy?"
Eliezer asked. "Did you
put rocks inside your
backpack?"

Eli laughed and
shook his head.

Next, Levi gave
Eliezer his green
backpack. Levi's bag felt like there were bricks
inside it. Eliezer then picked up Shimon's and
Moshe's backpacks and tried to walk.

Eliezer's back hurt. His shoulders hurt.
Even his legs hurt. It was so hard to walk.
He felt like he had a house on his back! What
was Eliezer to do? The bags were much heavier
than he ever imagined!

Eliezer could not ask his friends to carry their
own bags. After all, they had agreed to take
turns. So he started to walk ....

Then it happened. Eliezer couldn't help it.
As he was taking a step, he tripped and fell.

"Ahh!" yelled Eliezer, as he fell into a big
puddle. He got soaking wet! He tried not to get
the backpacks wet, too. But Levi's backpack
got wet. So did Moshe's and Eli's backpacks.
And they were so heavy that Eliezer could not
get up. Eli tried to help him. Levi tried, too.

But none of them could help Eliezer get up. The backpacks were just too heavy! Eliezer lay in the puddle.

Then two men came. They helped Eliezer up. They told him to go home quickly and change into dry clothing.

Levi, Moshe, Shimon and Eli went home, too. As Eliezer slowly walked home, he began to cry.

*Maybe my idea was not so great after all,* he thought. It isn't a good idea for any one of us to carry so many heavy bags. Our backpacks are much too heavy for anyone to carry all of them!

Eliezer made a decision. He decided to carry his own bag from then on. He liked his friends too much to watch them have such a hard time. Until he had to carry all the bags, he didn't realize how difficult it would be.

When he woke up the next morning, Eliezer ran quickly to his backpack. He picked it up and put it on his back. And do you know what? It didn't feel as heavy anymore.

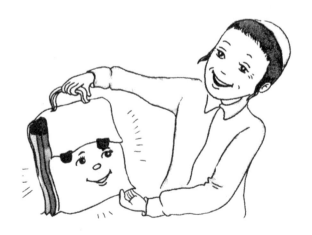

# CHAPTER 4

# The Shortcut

Every day, after school ends, Efrayim takes the bus home. The bus drops him off at his bus stop. It's only a few blocks from his home. He always runs straight home, so he can eat his snack and tell his mother about his day at school.

One day, Efrayim and his friend Yoni got

off the school bus at their usual stop. Efrayim was getting ready to say good-bye when Yoni stopped him.

"Wait, Efrayim," said Yoni. "I have something to show you. I know a great shortcut to your house."

"What's a shortcut?" Efrayim asked.

"A shortcut," Yoni explained, "is a fast

way to go from one place to another. I found a shortcut from the bus stop to your house yesterday. Do you want me to show you the shortcut now?"

"Sure!" Efrayim replied. "I always like to learn new things."

"Let's go," said Yoni. He picked up his backpack and began to walk.

Yoni led Efrayim through the playground and past some apartment buildings. Then they passed the grocery store, the shoe store and even Efrayim's favorite toy store.

"Look!" shouted Efrayim after a while. "There is my house! This shortcut made the walk home so much fun! Thank you for showing it to me."

Yoni smiled and said good-bye. Efrayim walked to his house alone.

"Ima, I'm home," Efrayim yelled, as he

raced toward the kitchen.

"Efrayim, where were you?" Ima asked. "I was worried about you. Why are you so late? I couldn't imagine what happened to you."

"Ima," Efrayim replied, "Yoni showed me a great shortcut! We had so much fun walking home together. I'm sorry you were worried. I didn't think about the time."

"Please, Efrayim," Ima said. "Please, don't do that again. I know you have a great time with Yoni, but I was worried. Please come straight home from school next time."

Efrayim agreed that he would do as his Ima asked.

A week later, Yoni told Efrayim about another great shortcut. Efrayim forgot about what his mother had told him.

This time, their shortcut took them through the nursery school playground. They passed rows of big houses Efrayim had never seen before. The boys walked for a long time. Soon Efrayim was getting tired and hungry. He remembered his mother was making chocolate chip cookies today and he couldn't wait to taste them.

"Are you sure you know where we're going?" Efrayim asked Yoni.

"Yes, I'm sure!" Yoni nodded.

But soon he looked less sure. "I think we're lost!" said Yoni. He looked like he was about to cry.

The boys sat down on a bench and tried to think of what to do. Efrayim covered his face with his hands. Yoni was so sad and scared that he started to cry.

Then an amazing thing happened. Yoni's

father drove by. When he saw the two boys sitting on the bench, he stopped his car. Yoni and Efrayim climbed into the car and Yoni's father drove them home. Yoni's father was not happy about Yoni's shortcut.

When Efrayim got home, he ran into the kitchen and gave his mother a big hug. His mother had been very worried. Efrayim was extremely late.

"Ima," Efrayim said, "I'm so sorry that I did not listen to what you told me! I'm sorry that I am late again. From now on you won't have to worry about my coming home late again! From now on, I will always come straight home after school!"

And that is exactly what Efrayim does. Now he always remembers what he told his Ima—even if his friends say they have the greatest idea. Every day, after school, he says good-bye to his friends and goes straight home.

CHAPTER 5

# Marbles for Everyone

Mordechai loves playing with marbles. His friends like playing with marbles, too. They play during recess. They play after school. They play whenever they can.

Everybody in Mordechai's family knows how much he loves marbles. For his birthday, his Zaidy gave Mordechai one of his favorite presents. He gave Mordechai a bag filled with fifty colorful marbles.

"Thank you so much, Zaidy!" Mordechai said excitedly. "I can't wait until recess tomorrow when I can show my new marbles to my friends!"

That night, Mordechai was so excited that he could hardly fall asleep. He did not want to let the marbles out of his sight. Finally, he became sleepy. He put all the marbles under his pillow. All night long, Mordechai dreamed about his new marbles.

The next morning, Mordechai woke up extra early. He washed *negel vasser*, dressed and grabbed his backpack. He put his new marbles into his backpack and ran to the front door.

"Where are you going, Mordechai?" Ima asked. "School doesn't start for another half an hour."

"I know, Ima," Mordechai replied, "but I want to get to school early today. Maybe I can play a game of marbles with one of my friends before school begins."

Mordechai's friend Menashe was already in the classroom when Mordechai arrived at school.

"Menashe, guess what!" said Mordechai. "My Zaidy gave me fifty new marbles for my birthday! Do you want to play with me before class starts?"

"Sure, why not?" Menashe replied.

The boys sat down on the floor in the back of the classroom and played. In just a few minutes, Mordechai won all twenty of Menashe's marbles.

"Yes!" shouted Mordechai. "Now I have seventy marbles! That's more than I ever had before!"

Menashe didn't answer. When Mordechai looked up, he saw that there were tears in Menashe's eyes.

"Why are you crying, Menashe?" Mordechai asked.

"I'm not crying," answered Menashe angrily. He picked up his blue backpack and walked toward his seat. "I just got some dust in my eyes."

Mordechai also went to his seat. Soon the rest of the boys and Rabbi Davis entered the room. Mordechai usually listened to every word his Rebbi said. But this time Mordechai didn't hear anything Rabbi Davis said. He was too busy thinking about all his marbles. He couldn't wait for recess to begin. He couldn't wait to win even more marbles! He imagined winning marbles from every boy in school! Soon he would have thousands, maybe millions, of marbles!

Time passed slowly for Mordechai. Finally, the recess bell rang.

"Who wants to play marbles?" Mordechai shouted, as he jumped out of his seat.

"I'll play," said Yossi. They went outside into the schoolyard and began to play.

Mordechai did well that day. He easily

won all of Yossi's twenty-five marbles. That meant that Mordechai now had a total of ninety-five marbles! He was jumping for joy!

Recess ended. Mordechai returned to his class. He was so busy thinking about winning all the marbles in the school that he didn't notice the look on his Rebbi's face.

"Children," Rabbi Davis said, "today at

recess I saw something that upset me."

"What was it, Rebbi?" Mordechai asked.

"I saw several sad children," he replied.

"Why? What happened?" Mordechai asked.

"They were sad because they lost all their marbles. Now they don't have anything to play with."

Mordechai thought about his friends Menashe and Yossi. They were not happy after they lost their marbles. Mordechai also could not play with them again because they had no marbles.

"I've decided to make a new rule," Rabbi Davis continued. "From now on, all marbles have to be returned at the end of any game. You can play as much as you want during recess. You can have fun. But at the end of recess, every boy should still have the same number of marbles. Do you understand?"

All of the boys nodded. Mordechai thought about what Rabbi Davis said. He knew that his friends were upset about losing their marbles. He knew that he should return Menashe's and Yossi's marbles. He wasn't happy about returning them. But he knew that his Rebbi was right.

As soon as class ended, Mordechai did what his Rebbi had asked. He slowly counted twenty marbles and gave them to Menashe. Then Mordechai counted out twenty-five marbles and returned them to Yossi. Menashe and Yossi thanked Mordechai. They were so happy! Now they had something to play with. When Mordechai saw how happy they were, he almost didn't care that he had to give up forty-five marbles. But he still felt that it would be great to have a lot of marbles.

The next day, Mordechai began to

understand how smart his Rebbi's rule was. He and his friend Avner were playing marbles during recess. They played for a long time. Avner kept winning Mordechai's marbles. By the end of recess, Mordechai's pockets were completely empty. He couldn't believe it. Avner had won all of Mordechai's fifty marbles.

*Oh, no!* thought Mordechai. He started to think what he would do now, with no marbles left.

"Don't be sad, Mordechai," said Avner. "Remember? The game was just for fun. Here are your marbles."

Avner returned all fifty marbles to Mordechai. Mordechai was so relieved that he decided that Rabbi Davis's rule was the smartest rule he ever heard of.

That night, when Mordechai's brothers showed each other all the marbles they had won from friends, Mordechai smiled. He knew he and his friends had won something even more important. It was much better to play the game for fun and then return the marbles you had won. This way, all the boys stayed happy and no one got upset.

It was just a game, after all!